W9-CMO-136

Waiting for Baby Joe

Waiting for Baby Joe

Pat Lowery Collins
Photographs by Joan Whinham Dunn

Albert Whitman & Company, Niles, Illinois

I'd like to express thanks to all the nurses in the Special Care Nursery at Nashua Memorial Hospital in Nashua, New Hampshire, especially to Cathy Hale, who facilitated the photo sessions there. Special thanks are also due to Kathy Teeple for her cooperation since the inception of this book. Her support group for the parents of premature infants, where she presented authorities in the field of neonatology, provided me with much useful information. I'm grateful as well to the parents themselves for sharing experiences, and to Dr. Colleen Collins at Boston City Hospital for providing additional technical advice. P.L.C.

Published in 1990 by Albert Whitman & Company
Published simultaneously in Canada by General Publishing, Limited, Toronto

Printed in the United States of America.
10 9 8 7 6 5 4 3 2 1

Library of Congress Cataloging-in-Publication Data

Collins, Pat Lowery.
Waiting for Baby Joe / Pat Lowery Collins; photographs by Joan Whinham Dunn.
p. cm.
Summary: Text and photographs describe what happens when Missy's brother, Joe, is born prematurely and needs special care in the hospital, disrupting family routines and causing Missy to feel confused and left out.
ISBN 0-8075-8625-0 (lib. bdg.)
[1. Babies—Fiction. 2. Brothers and sisters—Fiction.]
I. Dunn, Joan Whinham, ill. II. Title.
PZ7.C69675Wai 1990 *89-21457*
[E]—dc20 *CIP*
AC

The text of this book is set in Galliard.

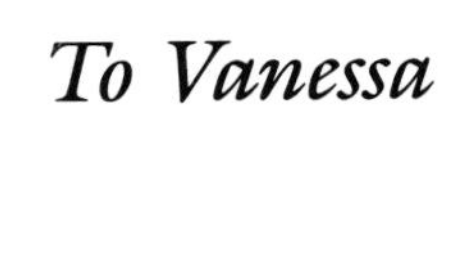

To Vanessa

"It can have my old baby shoes," Missy said.

She put her face against her mother's round belly and felt a big thump. "Or maybe my old sneakers."

"They'd be too big for its tiny bare feet," Missy's mother said. "Right now the baby is bare all over."

"But pretty soon it will need sneakers and a striped T-shirt," said Missy, "like Mary's baby."

Missy's friend, Mary, lived next door. She had a new baby brother.

"Well, not for awhile," said her mother. "When our baby needs clothes to keep warm, we'll have them ready. For now, it's warm inside of me."

Her mother rested her hands on her big stomach. "Only two more months to wait," she sighed.

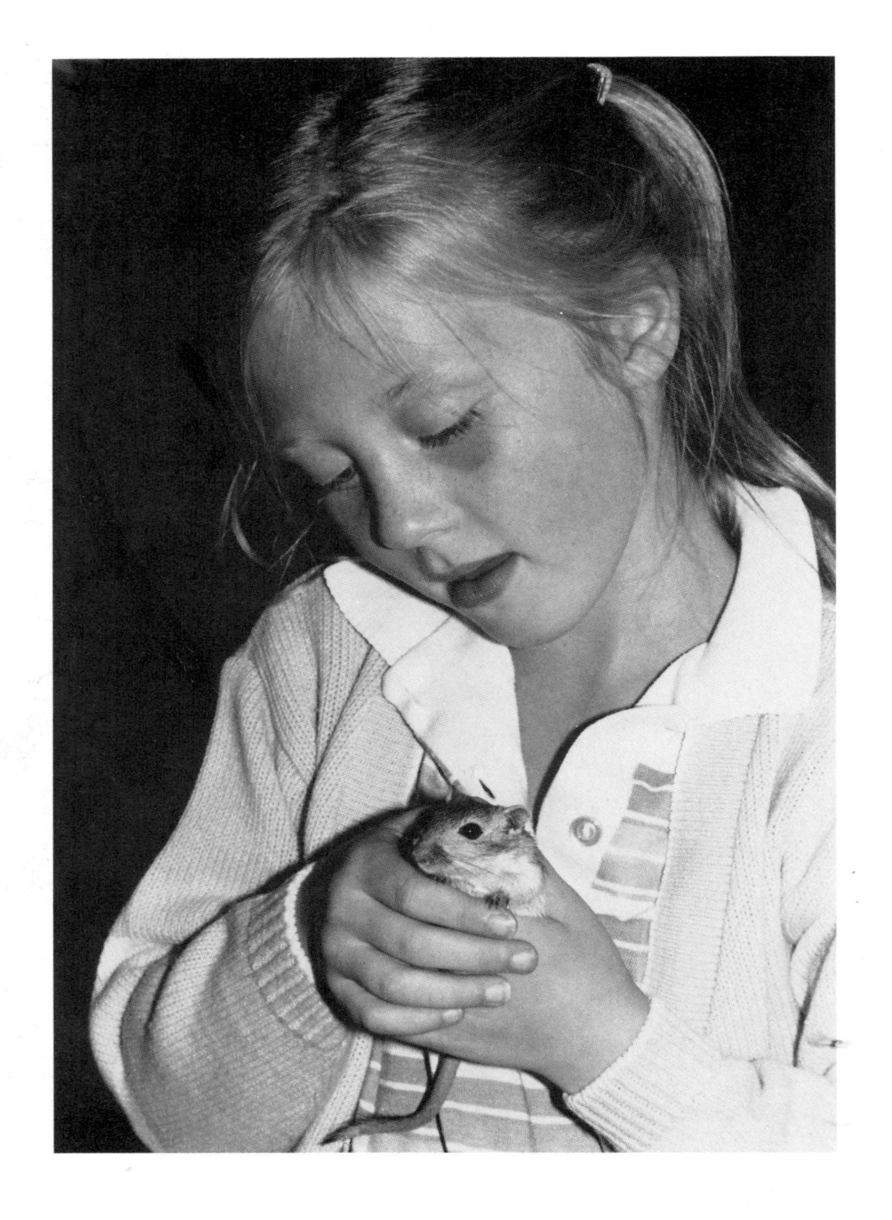

Missy had waited a week to get her pet gerbil. By the time it had come, she had almost forgotten about it. She knew that a month was four times longer than a week. How would she be able to wait for *two* whole months?

That night, Missy woke up and heard people talking.

"Go back to sleep," Gramma's voice said in the dark.

"Why are you here, Gramma?" whispered Missy.

Gramma pulled the blanket under Missy's chin. "I'm going to stay here with you," she said, "while your mother and father go to the hospital. The baby might be coming."

Missy rubbed her eyes. "But Mommy said he wouldn't be here for two more months."

"Sometimes babies come before they're supposed to," Gramma told her.

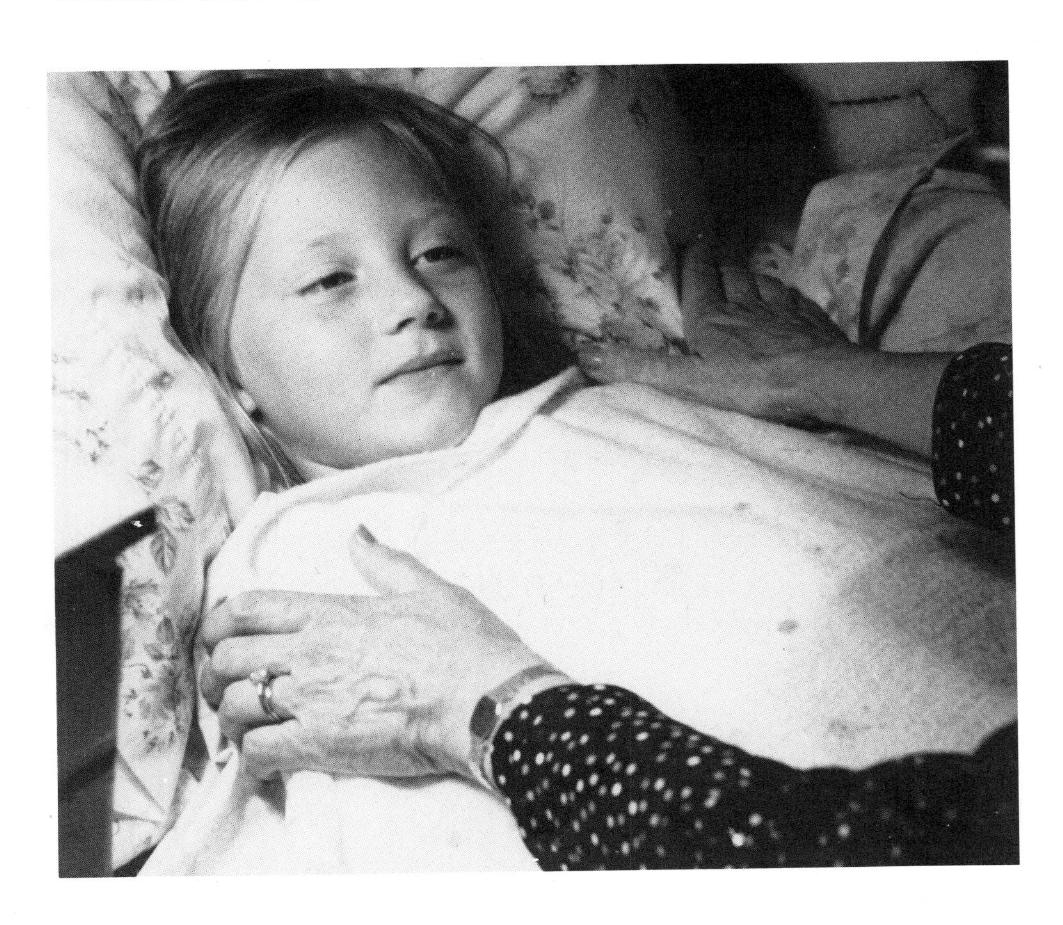

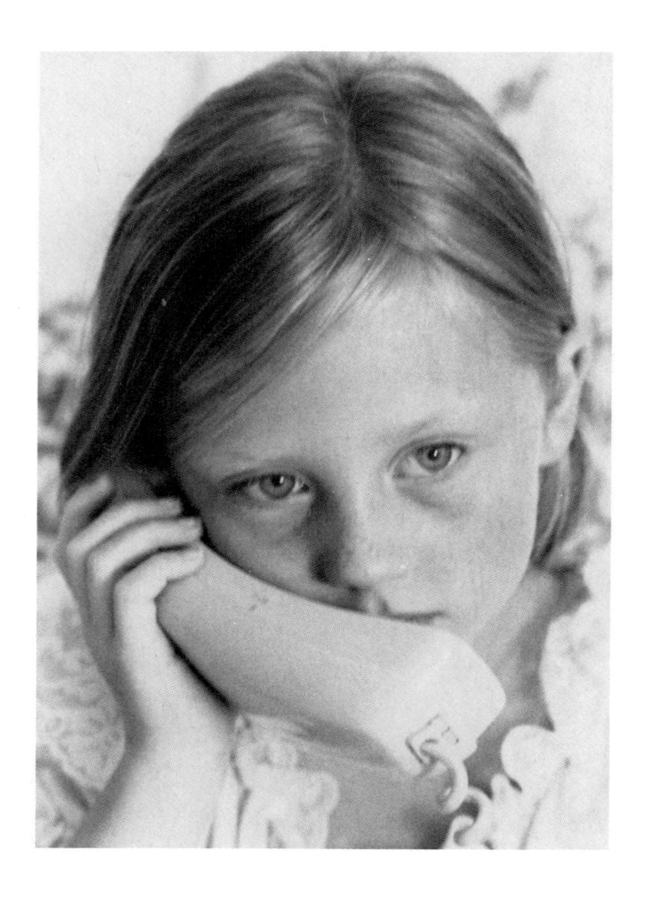

It was daylight when the telephone rang. Missy climbed out of bed and ran to the phone. It was Daddy.

"You have a new baby brother," he said.

"What's his name?" asked Missy. "Can you bring him right home?"

"His name is Joseph, but we'll call him Joe. I can't bring him home yet because he's so small."

"He was a big lump in Mommy," Missy said.

Gramma took the phone. "Is everything all right?"

She was silent for a long time.

Then she shouted, "Three pounds, two ounces!"

"Why did you yell like that?" Missy asked Gramma when she put the phone down.

"Because that's a real little baby!" she explained. "Why, he's only about half the size you were when you were born."

After breakfast, Mary came over to play with Missy.

"My mother had a baby that small once," Mary said.

"She did!" exclaimed Missy.

"But he got sick and died. He was premature like your baby."

"Oh," said Missy.

"What does *premature* mean, Gramma?" Missy asked after Mary went home.

"It means that the baby was born before he was ready to live outside of his mother's body, before he was old enough, or *mature*."

"Will Joe die?"

"I don't think so," said Gramma. "Today, doctors and nurses know just how to take care of very small babies."

"If he came home, I could take care of him," said Missy.

That afternoon, Daddy took Missy to the hospital.

On the way to her mother's room, they passed a room called a nursery. Through a big glass window, Missy could see lots of little beds with new babies wrapped in blankets. Some even had knitted hats on.

"To help keep them warm," Daddy explained to Missy.

Some babies were sleeping, and some were crying.

Missy looked at their red faces. "Boy, are they mad!" she said.

"They're just hungry or wet, or maybe they want to be held," Daddy told her.

"Where's Joe?" Missy wanted to know.

"He's in a different nursery," Daddy said. "You'll see."

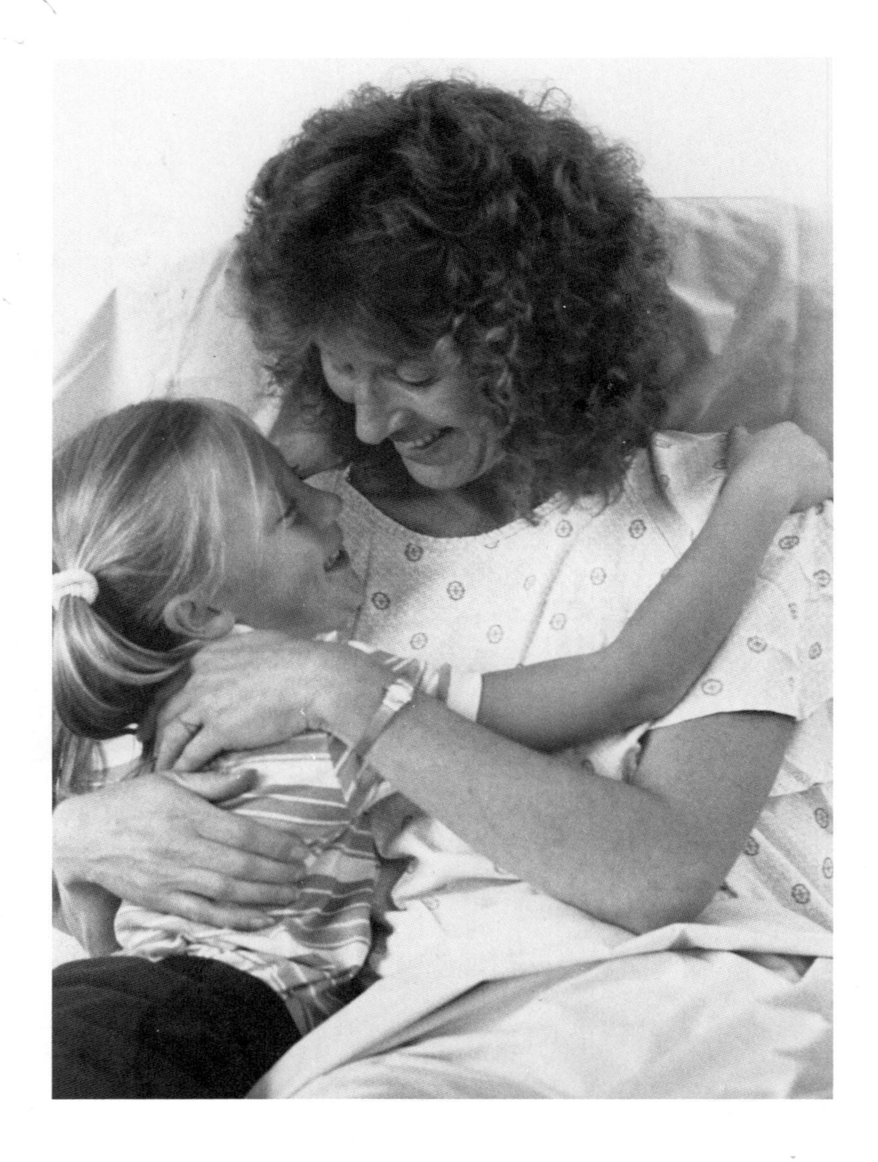

When Missy saw her mother, she wanted to jump right into bed with her. Missy woke her up with a kiss.

Her mother grinned and gave Missy a big hug. “I’ve missed you!” she said.

“Where’s your baby?” said Missy. “Where’s my brother?”

"Put on this clean coat, and we'll take a look," said the nurse.

"I'll come with you," said Missy's father.

They went to a nursery that wasn't so noisy. The beds were different. They were glass boxes with holes that could open and close.

"These are isolettes," the nurse explained. "They are safe, warm places for babies who are born too soon."

She pointed to one isolette. "There's Joe."

Joe's eyes were covered. His mouth twitched. Missy thought he looked like a frog.

"His head's too big," she said. "Why is the rest of him so small and skinny? He doesn't look anything like Mary's baby."

"His head will be growing slowly now," said the nurse, "but his body will grow faster. He should really still be

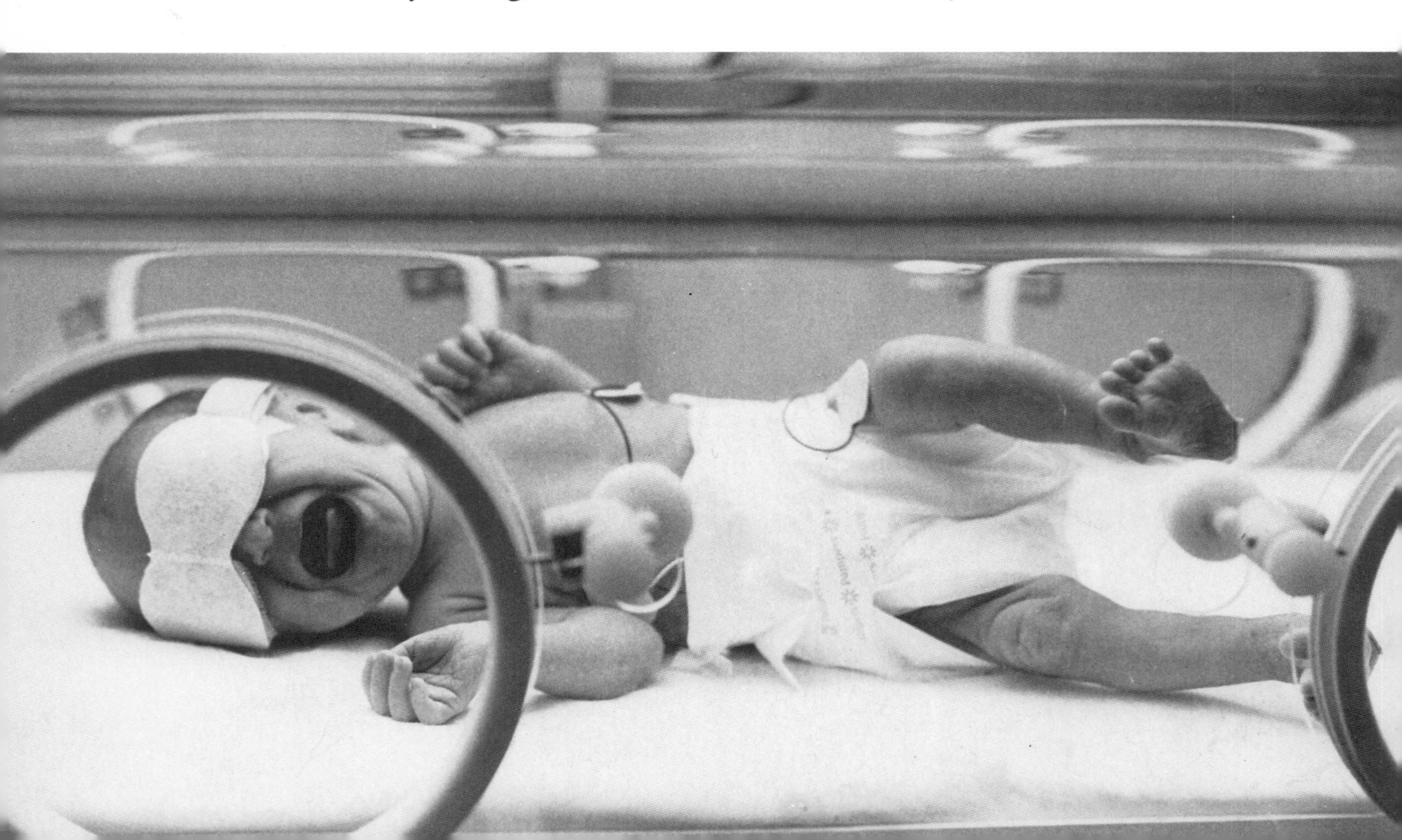

growing inside your mother. But he can't. So we sometimes feed him a special kind of food through a tube to help him grow."

"Why does he look so yellow?" asked Missy.

"There's something in Joe's blood that makes him look that way. The bright lights help to get rid of it. A part of Joe's body called the liver should do this. But it isn't mature enough yet."

"What are those patches for? I can't see his face."

"The patches protect Joe's eyes from the lights," said the nurse. "It's time to take them off now, and you can get a good look at him."

Missy watched the nurse flick the light switch and put her hand into the bed. She gently took off the patches. Then she turned Joe and stroked him.

"Would you like to hold your brother in the isolette like I'm doing?" she asked Missy.

Missy shook her head. Her doll, Betts, was about the size of Joe. Betts's arm came off once.

"He might break," she said.

"No, he wouldn't do that," said the nurse. "As long as you're gentle, you won't hurt Joe."

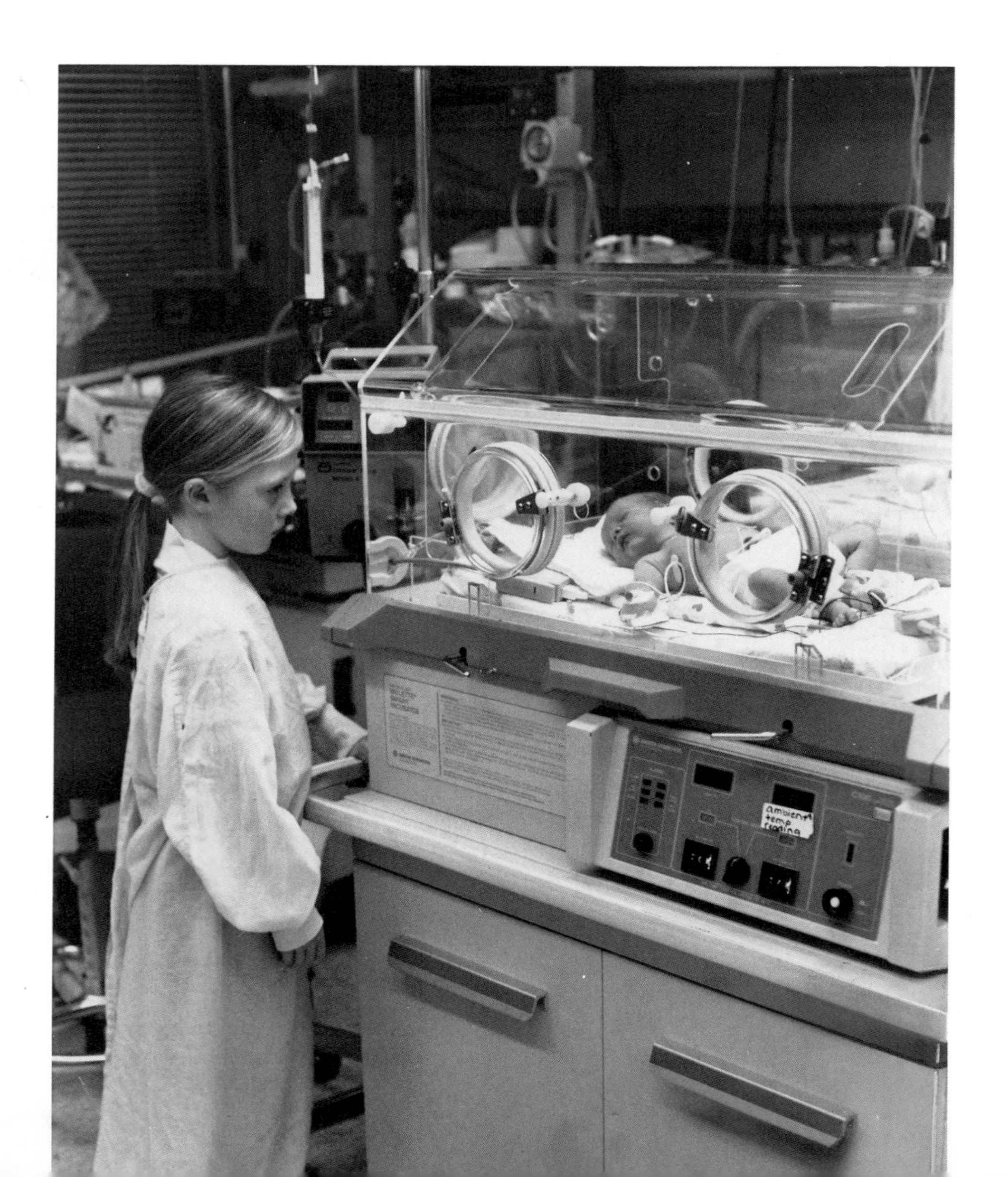

"Mommy was right," Missy told Gramma that night. "Joe is all bare. He needs some clothes now."

"He just needs a diaper in the isolette," said Gramma.

"But he'd look better with clothes on."

"He'll look better soon enough."

"I was a regular baby, right?"

"So is Joe. You looked like that once, but no one could see you. You were still inside your mother."

"I'm glad no one saw me looking like a scary frog."

Gramma laughed.

It seemed a long time to Missy before her mother came home. Her father said it had only been a few days. Joe wasn't with her, and Missy was happy she'd have her mother all to herself again. It would be just like before.

But it wasn't the same. Missy's mother took naps every little while.

And when Missy spilled her milk at dinner, her mother said, "Look at the mess you've made!" instead of, "We all spill things," like she used to.

"It was an accident," said Missy's father.

Her mother started to cry and left the room.

"Mommy's very tired," her daddy said. "It makes her grouchy."

"Maybe she's mad because her baby's so ugly," Missy said to herself. The words were louder than she'd meant them to be.

Daddy's face got tight. "She's sad, Missy, because Joe isn't at home with us."

Gramma came over often now, so that Missy's parents could go to the hospital. When Gramma couldn't come, Mary's sister, Jean, stayed with Missy.

"I can't find Missy anywhere!" Jean screamed into the phone one night. "I think she's run away!"

Missy's mother and father came rushing home from the hospital. They found Missy hiding under the piano.

"That was a terrible thing to do, Missy. You know how worried we've been about Joe," said her father.

"And were you worried about me?" asked Missy.

"Of course we were," said her mother. "What would we ever do without you!"

Missy was glad.

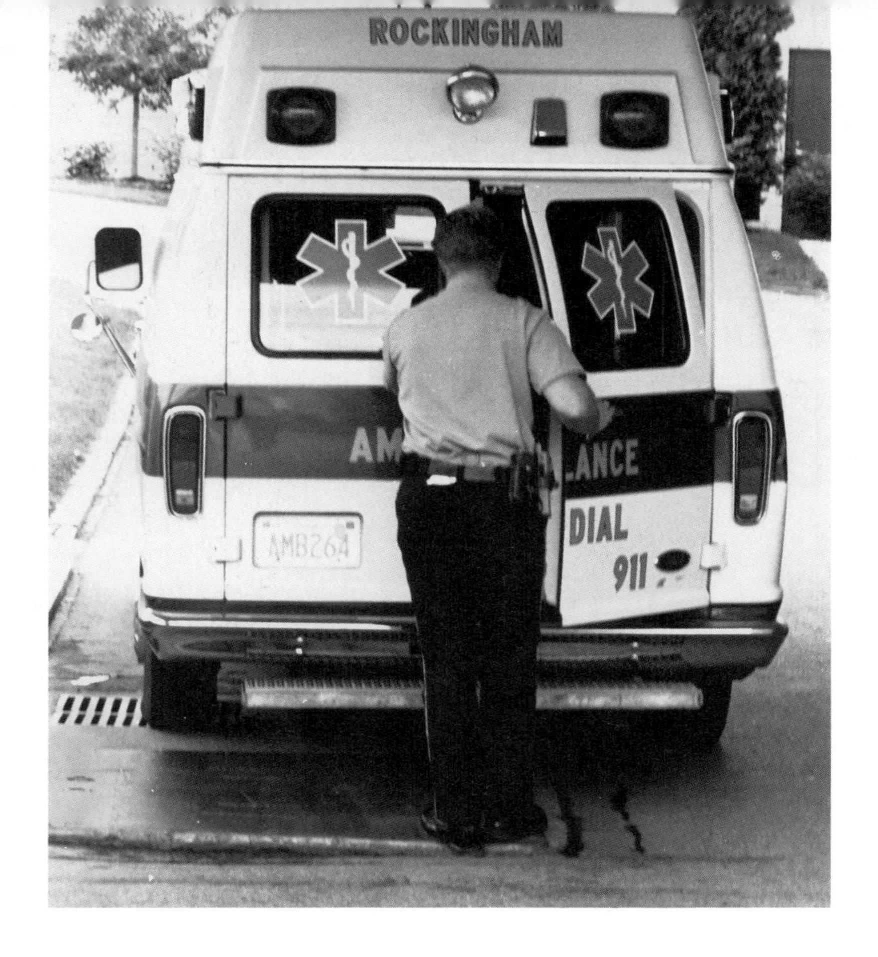

Missy sometimes worried about Joe, too. When she did, her parents would take her to the hospital to see him.

Once while they were visiting Joe, the doctor came in.

"I think it's time to move Joe to another hospital," he said, "where they have special tools to help him. Just like the rest of him," he added, "Joe's heart didn't finish forming. There is a place in it that didn't close. So now that he's stronger, we need to patch this small hole."

Missy and her father watched as an ambulance drove silently away with Joe and Missy's mother inside.

For awhile after that, it seemed to Missy that everyone talked in whispers.

But then one evening Missy's mother came home smiling.

"Joe's gaining weight," she said, "and his cheeks are almost rosy."

And it wasn't long before Missy's parents began to be home more often.

"Because Joe's doing so well," her mother said.

She didn't have to leave for the hospital as early each morning, and she was almost always home when Missy went to bed. Sometimes they even had time to play.

"Joe's coming home!" Gramma said in the middle of a very long day. Missy couldn't believe it.

Gramma said he weighed five pounds now, so Missy thought he'd be a big baby. But he wasn't. His fingers were like little pieces of curled macaroni. Even if he smiled, his eyes were usually closed. He was so quiet.

Once Missy thought he really looked at her. His eyes were wide open. But when she bent down next to him, he shut his eyes again. She was sure he didn't like her.

"He can't do anything but sleep or spit up," she grumbled. She poked at him, and he jumped.

"Do you think he's all right?" Gramma asked Missy's mother.

"The doctor says all premature babies sleep most of the time, and they startle easily." She didn't sound upset.

The doorbell rang.

It was Mary.

"My mom made me wait till your baby was home a few days. Can I see him now?" she asked.

"No," said Missy.

"Why? You got to see mine."

"Mine isn't ready yet."

One Saturday, Missy and her mother were eating lunch. Joe was sleeping in his infant seat on the sunny kitchen counter. He was so quiet that Missy almost forgot he was there. When she did look over at him, he had turned bluish at the tips of his fingers and toes and around his mouth.

Missy's mother jumped up and quickly flicked the bottoms of Joe's bare feet with her fingernail. Then she started to rub his back. He was as floppy as a rag doll. All at once, he gave a little gasp.

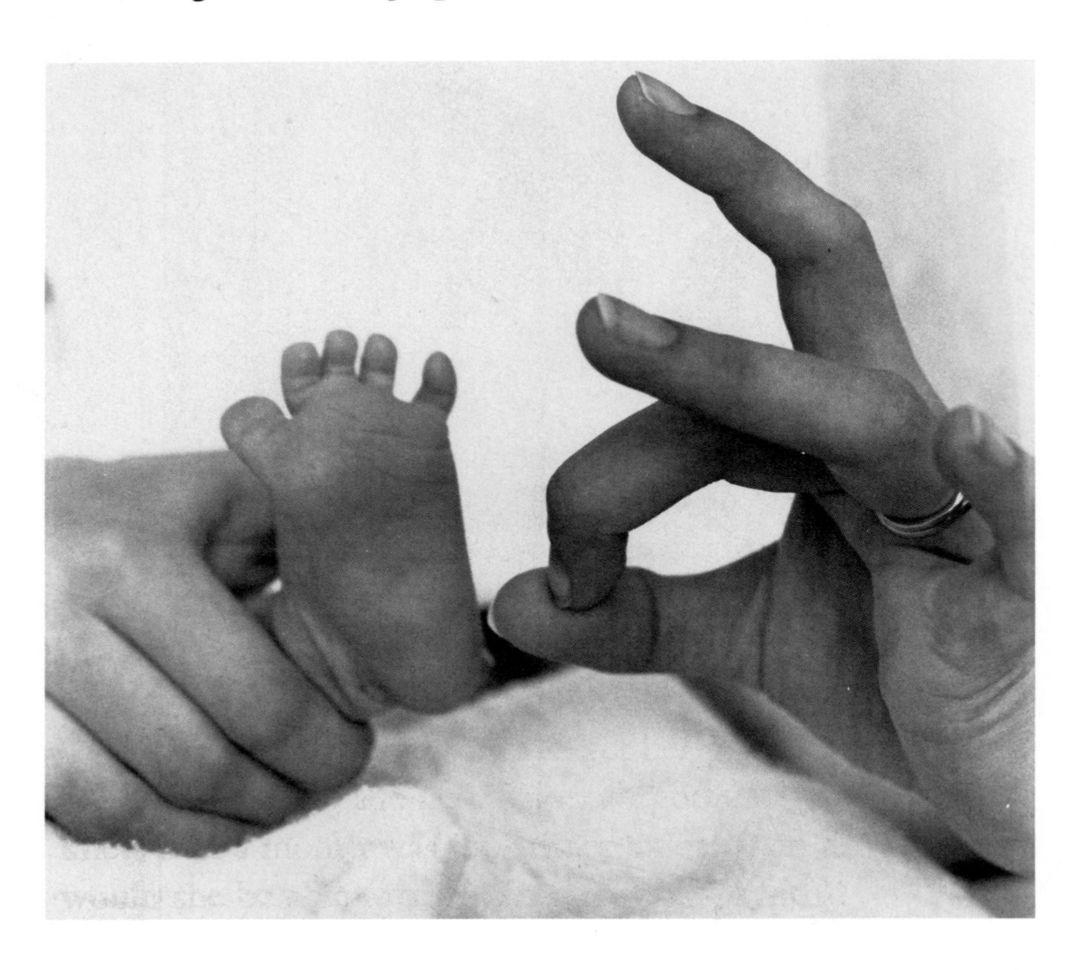

Missy's mother sat down hard in her chair. She held Joe until he started looking pinker again and making soft noises.

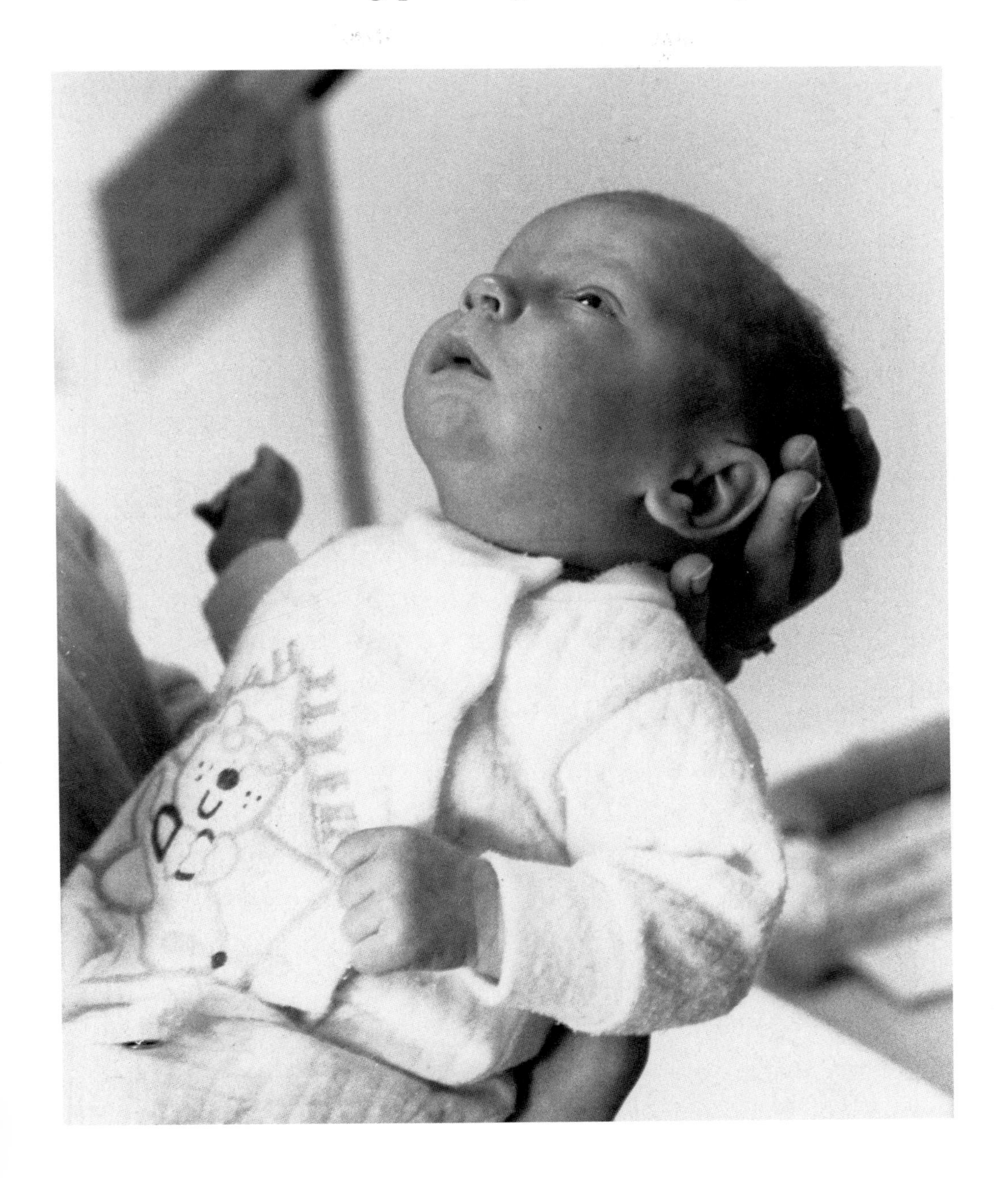

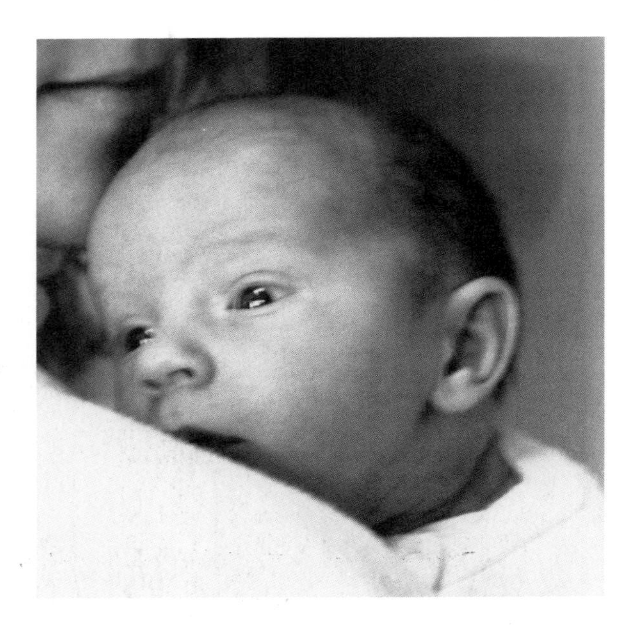

"Sometimes he forgets to breathe," she said in a shaky voice. Joe was still attached to a monitor to keep track of his breathing when someone wasn't in the room with him or at night. Missy didn't like seeing the wires from the small machine taped to Joe's skin. But her mother had explained that this was the way to make sure that he was all right.

"It will sound an alarm if there is any problem," she had added.

Missy hoped Joe wouldn't have trouble breathing again. One time the monitor beeped in the night, but her parents knew what to do to help Joe. After that, he didn't forget anymore.

And after awhile, he didn't jump so much. When he cried, his voice was louder than before. Missy's mother said that crying was Joe's way of telling them things.

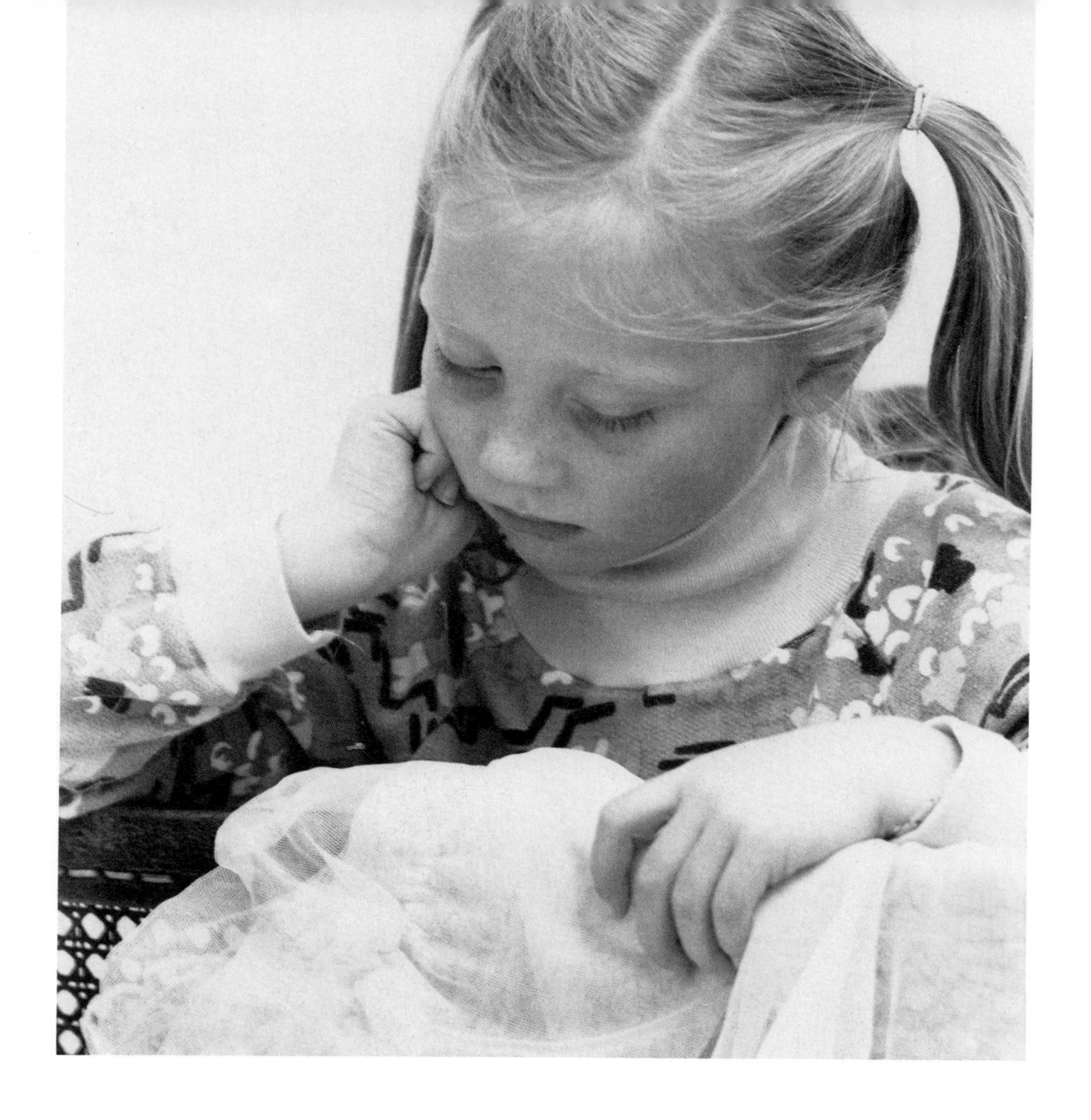

One afternoon, Joe began to cry louder than ever. When Missy came close to him, he looked at her and stopped crying. He didn't try to hide. He smiled.

"I think Joe is ready now!" Missy shouted at her mother over the noise of the vacuum cleaner.

"Ready for what?" her mother shouted back from inside the closet.

"Ready for a big sister!" Missy yelled. Her mother didn't seem to hear her. But Joe did, because he smiled again, and Missy was glad she had waited for him.

"O.K., Mary," Missy said into the phone. "You can see my baby in a few days." That would give her mother time to get Joe a striped shirt.

"Can't I come over right away?" asked Mary.

"A few days isn't a long time to wait," Missy told her. "You'll see."

Pat Lowery Collins was born in Los Angeles, California, where she had an early career as a child radio actress. A graduate of the University of Southern California, she has spent most of her adult life on the East Coast, where she and her husband, an engineering consultant, have raised five children.

Mrs. Collins is a poet and author of short stories as well as children's books. These include *My Friend Andrew; Tumble, Tumble, Tumbleweed; The River Shares Its Secret;* and *Taking Care of Tucker.* She is also a professional artist with paintings in both private and corporate collections.

Joan Whinham Dunn photographs people. A native of England, she has worked as a photojournalist for British newspapers and magazines and as a photograph editor for the *Times of Malta* and *Europe for Travellers.* Her career has taken her from photographic assignments with the British royal family to political crises in the Middle East. Her photographs have appeared in many international magazines and in travel and advertising media, and they have been exhibited in galleries in the United States and Britain.

Joan and her husband, a psychiatrist, make their home in an old farmhouse in New Hampshire. They have three children.